for Carol

Text copyright © 1978 by Richard Kennedy
Illustrations copyright © 1978 by Donna Diamond
All rights reserved
Printed in the United States of America

Library of Congress Cataloging in Publication Data

Kennedy, Richard.
The dark princess.

SUMMARY: A princess whose radiant beauty blinds her
and all who look upon her finds only one man willing to
submit to her test for suitors—the court fool.
[1. Princesses—Fiction] I. Diamond, Donna.
II. Title.
PZ7.K385Dar   [E]   78-1548
ISBN 0-8234-0329-7

The Dark Princess

written by Richard Kennedy
illustrated by Donna Diamond

Holiday House • New York

*T*HERE was a child born who was so beautiful that no one could look at her without blinking, and she was a Princess. Each day and each year she became more beautiful. When she was ten, those who spoke to her looked over her shoulder, or turned their heads while speaking. It was as if a great light shone out of her face. When she was a young lady and ready to marry, no one could look into her face at all. The sight would strike them blind. And another thing. The Princess herself was totally blind.

She was not born blind, but became blind year by year as she became more beautiful. The Royal Physician explained the matter to her parents, the King and Queen. He said the condition was caused by a "frontal optical reversal of the cognitive processes acting on the stereoscopic image-blending phenomenon which resulted in a transposed focal plane bilaterally projecting her sight into a dark area of her brain." He could put it more simply than this. "It is like a dark cloud that blocks out the sun. It could pass at any time."

And so, since it could pass at any time, the King and Queen kept her blindness a secret. That was easy enough to do, since it was impossible for anyone to look at the Princess directly, and a great, long-haired dog led her way and guarded her step, and she had the measure of every chair and table in the palace, and every bush and tree in the Royal Garden. Her ear was so clever that she knew the footstep of everyone on tile or on carpet, and their voices, of course. From the rustle of their clothes, she knew what others were wearing, and from the tinkle of metal and the clink of stone, their ornaments and jewelry, and no one could sit so quietly in a room that she would not know he was there.

One day, when the Princess was walking in the garden, the King made a wonderful discovery. He was standing at a stained glass window inside the palace as she passed, and his discovery was that he could look into her face through the dark glass and not be blinded. He called her and spoke to her face to face through the window and was awed by her beauty.

Everyone in the Kingdom who could afford it got himself a piece of colored glass to behold the Princess, and watched her come and go with her dog, her head held in a slight attentive cock, as if she were listening to music they could not hear, or pursuing some fancy in her mind. She carried herself with such aloofness that some thought she was conceited about her great beauty and could not bother to take notice of anyone else. Some said it was only modesty and a sign of good upbringing. But it was neither. She was merely counting her steps and listening to the many sounds that tell the way in total darkness, and feeling the trembling of the leash she held as the dog informed her of a chair or table out of place, a new-dug hole in the garden, a limb across a path, or anything else amiss or strange in her way. The people did not suspect she was blind.

Now this was the state of affairs when the first Prince came to the Kingdom to consider the girl for a bride, and through his glass—yes, even so darkly—she was as beautiful to him as anyone he had ever seen, and he loved her at once. After a while of courtly good manners, they walked in the garden alone, led by the Princess's dog. They stopped by a flowering bush, and the Prince looked at her through his glass and spoke.

"Forgive me," he said, "but this past hour has been an age to me, and there would be nothing left of me but dust if I would wait through a season of wooing to declare myself to you. Let me be plain and quick while I am not yet faded to a shadow by the sight of you. You are more beautiful than anyone I have ever seen or could imagine, and I am helplessly in love with you already."

"Are you?" said the Princess, touching a blossom.

"Forsooth," said the Prince, "my very self with love has leaped from me. I have forgotten who I am, in love. I would not know my face in a mirror. Marry me. Come with me and be my Queen, or say no to me and tell me my name so I may despair over the sound of it forever."

The Princess had been told that the Prince was handsome and well set up, and she had no reason to doubt it. His speech was fair (though a bit extravagant), his manners pleasant, and his voice sounded sweet to her.

"If you love me," said the Princess, "then you may prove it to me."

The Prince dropped to one knee. "Only tell me how," he said. "Any vow, any venture, any danger, any dare . . ."

"Look at me," said the Princess.

"What?"

"Take away your piece of colored glass and look at me directly."

"But . . . but . . ." the Prince stammered, getting to his feet again. "They say that, that if one does . . ."

"Yes," said the Princess, "if you do, you will be blinded."

"But to be *blind!*" said the Prince. "How awful. Certainly you wouldn't want me to be blind! Sight is more valuable than anything but life itself. How could you love me then?"

"Only then *could* I love you. Then I would believe that you truly loved me, and I would love you."

The Prince protested such an outrageous test of his love, and drew upon arguments from philosophy, law, physics, chemistry, and astronomy to declare the reasons why he could not meet the test. "Give me another test," he demanded.

"There is no other," said the Princess, and plucking a blossom she turned and walked back to the palace.

The Prince rode away that same day, and the King came to the Princess in her rooms and said, "Did the Prince not please you?"

"He pleased me well enough," she said, brushing the dog with long sweeping strokes, "and I might have loved him."

"But then why did he leave?" asked the King.

"Because he could not love *me*, father."

"Ye gods, he must have been blind! Excuse me, dear."

"No, he was not blind," said the Princess. "He would have hated that."

And so for a year the princes came, and each in his manner, shy or bold, plain or poetic, declared he had lost his heart in love for the Princess. But none would lose their sight for it, and all of them went away in a silent and puzzled wonder.

Likewise were the King and Queen puzzled. Princes were now coming from very far away, and soon there would be none left at all to come. They wondered—had the princes suspected that the girl was blind? The King and Queen had chosen to keep this a secret, and did not consider it so very unfair since the girl was likely to regain her sight at any moment. And besides, her blindness was a small thing in comparison to her beauty. They simply could not understand. Of course, they did not know of the test the girl proposed. And none could pass that test.

The Princess by this time had satisfied herself that she would not marry, and in these later days she became sad. It was not so much that she was sad because she would not have a husband, for those who do not marry can be happy, but her sadness was in her doubt that there was such a thing as love in the world. So many had told her that they loved her, but none of them would prove it in the way she asked. Then what was this love they spoke about? She was tired of the word.

The Princess walked more slowly than usual now, and sometimes she sat by a window for hours without moving, and she took no delight in stories or music, and if dessert had not been served after supper, she would not have noticed. It is a bad sadness to believe that there is no love in the world, and people have hanged themselves for less gloomy discoveries.

But it was worse yet than that. Believing that there was no love in the world was her lesser sorrow. Her greater sorrow was this: what if a Prince *should* give up his eyesight out of love for her? What had she to give in return? She was already blind. Just one time there was a Prince who had paused thoughtfully when she told him the test, and for a terrible few throbbing moments she feared that this one would actually go blind for her, and a strange agony rose in her breast, and she was relieved when the Prince began his protest.

Later and alone, the poor girl concluded that her fear and agony in those moments was of the reason that even though there may be love in the world, there was no love in herself. She had nothing to give to prove it. That was her greater sorrow. She believed she could not love.

When her thoughts followed along these dismal lines for too long a time, and she found herself wondering how it would feel to fall from the great tower, and how long it would take before she was broken on the ground, the Princess shook her head and hurried to the kitchen to have a picnic packed for herself, and she took herself away from her thoughts of oblivion, out through the garden and beyond the great stone lion gates on the path that went down to the ocean. Her dog led the way, and as the surf grew louder in the distance and the first smell of salt air came to her, she hummed a tune to raise her spirits. Only the sea was large enough to fill the emptiness she sometimes felt inside herself, and there at the edge of the land where a cliff dropped into the crashing surf below, she would eat her picnic lunch and drink a glass of wine, and sometimes she would smile.

On this day there was someone else out on a picnic at that place. The Court Fool was sitting with his legs dangling over the side of the cliff, and next to him was a bottle of wine and some chicken bones. The dog barked, and the Fool turned to look. He blinked, and quickly got out his piece of colored glass and watched the Princess approach. As usual, she seemed to take no notice of him at all, and it was not his place to greet her first. What a strange, distracted girl she seemed to be, and he concluded that she was probably caught up in a daydream. In fact, she came walking out onto the cliff so purposefully and yet so much like a sleepwalker, that he was certain she was going to walk right over the edge, and he called, "Look out!"

Hardly were the words out of his mouth when she stopped.

"Look out?" she said, turning toward him but looking over his head. "Look out for what? I am exactly five steps from the edge of the cliff." She had recognized his voice, of course. "What are you doing out here, Fool?"

"Well, as you see, Princess, I came for a little picnic like yourself. Roast chicken, a little wine. Will the dog eat the bones?"

"You are certainly a fool if you don't know that chicken bones are dangerous for dogs," she said, and she spread out a cloth to set her picnic basket on. The Fool raked the bones over the side and watched them fall into the surf below. He looked at the Princess again through his colored glass, then took a drink of his wine. He had never been so close to her before, and certainly he had never been alone with her. What could he say? He ventured a common subject: "They say another Prince is coming to visit next week, from very far away."

"I have heard that," said the Princess, breaking some bread and putting a piece of cheese in her mouth. "It matters little."

The Fool had intended to follow up on such a conversation, for he was safe and in his place to talk of the visiting princes, their fine dress and horses, and to gossip of neighboring king-doms, but instead he said, "Why don't you ever laugh at me?"

The Princess stopped chewing. She started to make a stern face at the Fool, but then she shrugged. "I do laugh, now and again." The truth was, of course, that she had never been able to see his funny antics when he entertained at court, and remembered to laugh only sometimes, when the others laughed.

"No you don't laugh, not really," said the Fool, "and I am a student of laughing. No, you don't laugh, not like the others. And the others laugh when I see them about the hallways and do a face and a little step for them, but you seem to ignore me."

The Princess folded some ham into her bread. "Perhaps you are not such a funny fool as you think you are."

The Fool plucked at the grass and sprinkled it into the wind blowing up past his legs. "I would think my face was funny enough," he said, and they sat and listened to the ocean. "But I *can* make you laugh," said the Fool at last. "Yes, I could make you laugh this very moment if I wanted to."

"I guarantee you cannot," said the Princess, and she smiled. "Stand on your head, stretch out your cheeks and ears, look at me under your legs, and squash your nose. You couldn't make me laugh."

"Then I will, just to show you," said the Fool. "And I will do it with words alone. Be ready to laugh, now, for here it is that will amuse you greatly, and only three words will do it." He took a double gulp of wine and then said, "I love you."

The Princess did not laugh. She lowered her head and gazed very solemnly toward the ground. Presently she said, "Yes, for a fool to love a Princess—I suppose that might be funny. However, since it isn't true, it isn't funny. Twoscore princes have come and gone, and all of them said that they loved me. But none of them did, and you do not, either."

The Princess poured herself a glass of wine and took a sip. "There is no such thing as love, and that's why I don't laugh at you now, and why I rarely laugh. What you think you love you do not, really. I am only beautiful, and if you lost the way to see me, you would not love me."

"No," he said. "It is not your beauty I love, it is *you* I love, it is your *ways* I love. A fool may look closely to know who a person is, and with little insult, for he need only wag his nose to be excused. And though I have seen you only darkly, I have seen you deeply, and it is you yourself that I love."

Now the Princess did laugh. "Let me tell you something. Will you promise to keep it a secret?"

"In my heart," said the Fool. And so the Princess told him why she had not chosen a Prince to marry, and how she had put her test to them, and how they all had declined to look at her directly and go blind for their love.

"I would be blind for you," said the Fool.

The Princess gathered up her things and put them in the basket. "Then you would be a fool for sure." She folded her picnic cloth and stood up. "Yes, you would be the best fool of all. Any of the princes would have had me for a bride upon looking at me directly. But I cannot marry you, and you would have nothing for it but darkness."

The Fool smiled to himself and nodded. Then he too stood up next to her and looked at her through his colored glass. The Princess could feel the Fool's sadness, and she spoke again before turning to leave.

"You are a good and fortunate fool to believe in love, but your sadness is not as great as it could be. Mine is greater. Remember, I do not believe in love."

"But you *must* believe in love," said the Fool. "I would go blind that you do, for that alone I would go blind."

And then the Princess was reminded of her greater sorrow —her sorrow that even though another might one day give his sight out of love for her, she had nothing to give in return. She shook her head.

"Ah, dear Fool, we could be certain of nothing except that you would be blind. How could I believe? I have nothing to give in return. But here, let me touch your hand before I go."

The Princess reached out her hand, and she felt a thin, smooth object placed in her palm. She caught her breath to cry out, but the Fool cried, "Oh, oh . . ." and she heard him stumble backwards, and heard his foot slide on the cliff's edge. He fell without a sound, and she heard him splash in the surf below. She dropped the picnic basket and the piece of colored glass, touched her toe to the edge of the cliff, and leaped into the water to save him, for he was only newly blind.

And there in the darkness below they touched for a moment, and then they drowned.

And in that moment they touched, the sun rose a million times for them, and the Princess and the Fool could see each other and all the things of life and the world more clearly than but a dozen people since the beginning of time. And that moment they touched outlasted the life of the King and Queen, and outlasted the life of the Kingdom. And that moment they touched is lasting still, and will outlast us, too.